The Adventures of CAPTAIN UNDERPANTS

NOW IN FULL COLOUR

TRA-LA-LAAAA!

The First Epic Novel by

DAV PILKEY

with colour by Jose Garibaldi

For David and Nancy Melton with gratitude

Scholastic Children's Books
An imprint of Scholastic Ltd
Euston House, 24 Eversholt Street
London, NW1 1DB, UK
Registered office: Westfield Road, Southam,
Warwickshire, CV47 0RA
SCHOLASTIC and associated logos are trademarks
and/or registered trademarks of Scholastic Inc.

First published in the US by Scholastic Inc, 1997
First published in the UK by Scholastic Ltd, 2000

This edition published 2014

Copyright © Dav Pilkey, 1997

The right of Dav Pilkey to be identified as the author
of this work has been asserted by him.

ISBN 978 1407 14395 8

A CIP catalogue record for this book is available from the British Library.

Printed and bound in Italy
Papers used by Scholastic Children's Books are made from
wood grown in sustainable forests.

1 3 5 7 9 10 8 6 4 2

www.scholastic.co.uk

Be sure to check out Dav Pilkey's
Extra-Crunchy web site
O' Fun at www.pilkey.com

Sturgeon General's Warning:
Some material in this book may be
considered offensive by people
who don't wear underwear.

CHAPTERS

CHAPTER 1
GEORGE AND HAROLD

Meet George Beard and Harold Hutchins.
George is the kid on the left with the tie
and the flat-top. Harold is the one on the
right with the T-shirt and the bad haircut.
Remember that now.

George and Harold were best friends. They had a lot in common. They lived right next door to each other and they were both in the same fourth-grade class at Jerome Horwitz Elementary School.

George and Harold were usually responsible kids. Whenever anything bad happened, George and Harold were usually responsible.

But don't get the wrong idea about these two. George and Harold were actually very nice boys. No matter what everybody else thought, they were good, sweet, and lovable. . . Well, OK, maybe they weren't so sweet and lovable, but they were good nonetheless.

It's just that George and Harold each had a "silly streak" a *kilometre* long. Usually that silly streak was hard to control. Sometimes it got them into trouble. And once it got them into big, *BIG* trouble.

But before I can tell you that story, I have to tell you *this* story.

CHAPTER 2
TREE HOUSE COMIX, INC.

After a hard day of cracking jokes, pulling pranks, and causing mayhem at school, George and Harold liked to rush to the old tree house in George's backyard. Inside the tree house were two big old fluffy chairs, a table, a cupboard crammed with junk food, and a padlocked crate filled with pencils, pens, and stacks and stacks of paper.

9

Now, Harold loved to draw, and George loved to make up stories. And together, the two boys spent hours and hours writing and drawing their very own comic books.

Over the years, they had created hundreds of their own comics, starring dozens of their own superheroes. First there was "Dog Man", then came "Timmy the Talking Toilet", and who could forget "The Amazing Cow Lady"?

But the all-time greatest superhero they ever made up *had* to be "The Amazing Captain Underpants".

George came up with the idea.

"Most superheroes *look* like they're flying around in their underwear," he said. "Well, this guy actually *is* flying around in his underwear!"

The two boys laughed and laughed.

"Yeah," said Harold, "he could fight with *Wedgie Power*!"

George and Harold spent entire afternoons writing and drawing the comic adventures of Captain Underpants. He was their coolest superhero ever!

Luckily for the boys, the secretary at Jerome Horwitz Elementary School was much too busy to keep an eye on the photocopier machine. So whenever they got a chance, Harold and George would sneak into the office and run off several hundred copies of their latest Captain Underpants adventure.

After school, they sold their homemade comics on the playground for 50¢ each.

THE ReaLLY COOL Adventures OF
CAPTAIN UNDERPANTS
WRitten by George Beard• Drawed by Harold Hutchins
It WAS A time of darkness And Dispare for PLanet earth. Bad guys had taken over the Streets, and aLL of the superherose in the world were too old to Fight evil.
Hey
Ha Ha
Then aLong came a new improved extra-strength super hero.
TRa-La-Laaaa!
Look up in the sky. it's A Bird.
it's A PLane
it's A egg-saLad Sandwich.
No way! I'm captain UNDERPANTS

So CAPTAIN UNDERPANTS took off RUNning. the Inedible HUNK chased him.
GRRR
Heeelp!
And chased him...
and chased him.
FinaLy the InediBLe HUNK got too Tired and thirsty to cHase CAPTAIN UNderpants.
Boys
How ABOUT A NiSe drink of WATer?

CHAPTER 4

MEAN OLD MR KRUPP

Do you see that old guy looking out the window up there?

That's Mr Krupp, the principal.

Now, Mr Krupp was the meanest,
sourest old principal in the whole history
of Jerome Horwitz Elementary School. He
hated laughter and singing. He hated the
sounds of children playing at break-time.
In fact, he hated children altogether!

And guess which two children Mr
Krupp hated most of all?

If you guessed George and Harold,
you're right! Mr Krupp *hated* George and
Harold.

He hated their pranks and their wise-
cracks. He hated their silly attitudes and
their constant giggling. And he especially
hated those awful *Captain Underpants*
comic books.

"I'm going to get those boys one day,"
Mr Krupp vowed. "One day very, very
soon!"

KNEEL
HERE

CHAPTER 5
ONE DAY VERY,
VERY SOON

Remember when I said that George and Harold's "silly streak" got them into big, *BIG* trouble once? Well, this is the story of how that happened. And how some huge pranks (and a little blackmail) turned their principal into the coolest superhero of all time.

It was the day of the big football game between the Horwitz Knuckleheads and the Stubinville Stinkbugs. The stands were filled with fans.

The cheerleaders ran on to the field and shook their pom-poms over their heads.

A fine black dust drifted out of their pom-poms and settled all around them.

"Gimme a K!" shouted the cheerleaders.

"*K!*" repeated the fans.

"Gimme an N!" shouted the cheerleaders.

"*N!*" repeated the fans.

"Gimme an . . . a-ah-ah-A-CHOO!" sneezed the cheerleaders.

"*A-ah-ah-A-CHOO!*" repeated the fans.

The cheerleaders sneezed and sneezed
and sneezed some more. They couldn't
stop sneezing.

"Hey!" shouted a fan in the stands.
"Somebody sprinkled black pepper into
the cheerleaders' pom-poms!"

"I wonder who did that?" asked
another fan.

The cheerleaders stumbled off the field, sneezing and dripping with mucus, as the marching band members took their places.

But when the band began to play, steady streams of bubbles began blowing out of their instruments! Bubbles were *everywhere*! Up and down the field the marching band slipped and slid, leaving behind a thick trail of wet, bubbly foam.

"Hey!" shouted a fan in the stands. "Somebody poured bubble bath into the marching band's instruments!"

"I wonder who did that?" asked another fan.

Soon, the football teams took the field. The Knuckleheads kicked the ball. Up, up, up went the ball. Higher and higher it went. The ball sailed into the clouds and kept right on going until nobody could see it any more.

"Hey!" shouted a fan in the stands. "Somebody filled the game ball with *helium*!"

"I wonder who did that?" asked another fan.

But the missing ball didn't make any difference because at that moment, the Knuckleheads were rolling around the field, scratching and itching like crazy.

"Hey!" shouted the coach. "Somebody replaced our Deep-Heating Muscle Rub Lotion with Mr Prankster's Extra-Scratchy Itching Cream!"

"We wonder who did that?!" shouted the fans in the stands.

The whole afternoon went on much the same way, with people shouting everything from "Hey, somebody put Sea-Monkeys in the lemonade!" to "Hey, somebody glued all the bathroom doors shut!"

Before long, most of the fans in the stands had gotten up and left. The big game had been forfeited, and everyone in the entire school was *miserable*.

Everyone, that is, except for two
giggling boys crouching in the shadows
beneath the stands.

"Those were our best pranks yet!"
laughed Harold.

"Yep," chuckled George, "they'll be
hard to top, that's for sure."

"I just hope we don't get busted for
this," said Harold.

"Don't worry," said George. "We
covered our tracks really well. There's
no way we'll get busted!"

CHAPTER 6
BUSTED

The next day at school, an announcement came over the loudspeakers.

> "George Beard and Harold Hutchins, please report to Principal Krupp's office at once."

"Uh-oh!" said Harold. "I don't like the sound of *that*!"

"Don't worry," said George. "They can't prove anything!"

George and Harold entered Principal Krupp's office and sat down on the chairs in front of his desk. The two boys had been in this office together countless times before, but this time was different. Mr Krupp was *smiling*. As long as George and Harold had known Mr Krupp, they had never, *ever* seen him smile. Mr Krupp knew something.

"I didn't see you boys at the big game yesterday," said Mr Krupp.

"Uh, no," said George. "We weren't feeling well."

"Y-Y-Yeah," Harold stammered nervously. "W-W-We went home."

"Aw, that's too bad," said Principal Krupp. "You boys missed a good game."

George and Harold quickly glanced at each other, gulped, and tried hard not to look guilty.

"Lucky for you, I have a videotape of the whole thing," Mr Krupp said. He turned on the television in the corner and pressed the play button on the VCR.

A black-and-white image appeared on the TV screen. It was an overhead shot of George and Harold sprinkling pepper into the cheerleaders' pom-poMs Next came a shot of George and Harold pouring liquid bubble bath into the marching band's instruments.

"How do you like the *pre-game show*?" asked Mr Krupp with a devilish grin.

George eyed the television screen in terror. He couldn't answer. Harold's eyes were glued to the floor. He couldn't look.

The tape went on and on, revealing all of George and Harold's "behind the scenes" antics. By now, both boys were eyeing the floor, squirming nervously, and dripping with sweat.

Mr Krupp turned off the TV.

"You know," he said, "ever since you boys came to this school, it's been one prank after another. First you put dissected frogs in the Jell-O salad at the parent-teacher banquet. Then you made it snow in the cafeteria. Then you rigged all the intercoms so they played "Weird Al" Yankovic songs *full blast* for six hours straight.

"For *four long years* you two have been running amok in this school, and I've never been able to prove anything – until now!"

Mr Krupp held the videotape in his hand. "I took the liberty of installing tiny video surveillance cameras all around the school. I knew I'd catch you two in the act one day. I just didn't know it would be *so easy*!"

CHAPTER 7
A LITTLE BLACKMAIL

Mr Krupp sat back in his chair and chuckled to himself for a long, long time. Finally, George got up the courage to speak.

"W-What are you going to do with that tape?" he said.

"I thought you'd never ask," laughed Principal Krupp.

"I've thought long and hard about what to do with this tape," Mr Krupp said. "At first, I thought I'd send copies to your parents."

The boys swallowed hard and sank deeply into their chairs.

"Then I thought I might send a copy to the school board," Mr Krupp continued. "I could get you both *expelled* for this!"

The boys swallowed harder and sank deeper into their chairs.

"Finally, I came to a decision," Mr Krupp concluded. "I think the football team would be very curious to find out just *who* was responsible for yesterday's fiasco. I think I'll send a copy to them!"

George and Harold leaped out of their chairs and fell to their knees.

"No!" cried George. "You can't do that. They'll *kill* us!"

"Yeah," begged Harold, "they'll kill us every day for the rest of our lives!"

Mr Krupp laughed and laughed.

"Please have mercy," the boys cried. "We'll do anything!"

"Anything?" asked Principal Krupp with delight. He reached into his desk, pulled out a list of demands, and tossed it at the boys. "If you don't want to be *dead as long as you live*, you'll follow these rules *exactly*!"

George and Harold carefully looked over the list.

"This . . . this is blackmail!" said George.

"Call it what you like," Principal Krupp snapped, "but if you two don't follow that list *exactly*, then this tape becomes the property of the Horwitz Knuckleheads!"

CHAPTER 8

CRIME AND PUNISHMENT

At six o'clock the next morning, George and Harold dragged themselves out of bed, walked over to Mr Krupp's house, and began washing his car.

Then, while Harold scrubbed the tyres, George roamed around the yard pulling up all the weeds and nettles he could find. Afterwards, they cleaned the gutters and washed all the windows on Mr Krupp's house.

At school, George and Harold sat up straight, listened carefully, and spoke only when spoken to. They didn't tell jokes, they didn't pull pranks – they didn't even smile.

Their teacher kept pinching herself. "I just *know* this is a dream," she said.

At lunch, the two boys vacuumed
Mr Krupp's office, shined his shoes,
and polished his desktop. At break, they
clipped his fingernails and ironed his tie.

Each spare moment in the boys' daily
schedule was spent catering to Mr Krupp's
every whim.

After school, George and Harold mowed Mr Krupp's lawn, tended his garden, and began painting the front of his house. At sunset, Mr Krupp came outside and handed each boy a stack of books.

"Gentlemen," he said, "I've asked your teachers to give you *both* extra homework. Now go home, study hard, and I'll see you back here at six o'clock tomorrow morning. We've got a busy day ahead of us."

"Thank you, sir," moaned the two boys.

George and Harold walked home dead tired.

"Man, this was the worst day of my entire life," said George.

"Don't worry," said Harold. "We only have to do this for eight more years. Then we can move away to some far-off land where they'll never find us. Maybe Antarctica."

"I've got a better idea," said George.

He took a piece of paper out of his pocket and handed it to Harold. It was an old magazine ad for the 3-D Hypno-Ring.

"How's *this* going to help us?" asked Harold.

"All we gotta do is hypnotize Mr Krupp," said George. "We'll make him give us the video and forget this whole mess ever happened."

"That's a great idea!" said Harold. "And the best part is we only have to wait four-to-six weeks for delivery!"

CHAPTER 9
FOUR-TO-SIX
WEEKS LATER

After four-to-six weeks of backbreaking slave labour, gruelling homework assignments, and humiliating good behaviour at school, a package arrived in George's mailbox from the Li'l Wiseguy Novelty Company.

It was the 3-D Hypno-Ring.

"Hallelujah!" cried George. "It's everything I ever hoped for!"

"Let me see, let me see," said Harold.

"Don't look directly at it," warned George. "You don't want to get hypnotized, do you?"

"Do you really think it will work?" asked Harold. "Do you really think we can 'amaze our friends, control our enemies, and take over the world' just like the ad says?"

"It better work," said George. "Or else we just wasted four whole bucks!"

CHAPTER 10
THE 3-D HYPNO-RING

The next morning, George and Harold didn't arrive early at Mr Krupp's house to wash his car and reshingle his roof. In fact, they were even a little late getting to school.

When they finally showed up, Mr Krupp was standing at the front door waiting for them. And boy, was he *angry*!

Mr Krupp escorted the boys into his office and slammed the door.

"All right, where were you two this morning?" he growled.

"We wanted to come over to your house," said George, "but we were busy trying to figure out the secret of this *ring*."

"What ring?" snapped Mr Krupp.

George held up his hand and showed the ring to Principal Krupp.

"It's got one of those weird patterns on it," said Harold. "If you stare at it long enough, a picture appears."

"Well, hold it still," snarled Mr Krupp. "I can't see the darn thing!"

"I have to move it back and forth," said George, "or else it won't work."

Mr Krupp's eyes followed the ring back and forth, back and forth, back and forth, and back and forth.

"You have to stare deeper into the ring," said Harold. "Deeper . . . deeeper . . . deeeeper . . . deeeeeeeeeper."

"You are getting sleepy," said George. "Veeeeery sleeeeeeeeepy."

Mr Krupp's eyelids began to droop. "I'mmmsssooooosssleeepy," he mumbled.

After a few minutes, Mr Krupp's eyes were closed tight, and he began to snore.

"You are under our spell," said George. "When I snap my fingers, you will obey our every command!"

Snap!

"Iwwilllloobeyyy," mumbled Mr Krupp.

"All right," said George. "Have you still got that videotape of me and Harold?"

"Yeeessss," mumbled Mr Krupp.

"Well, hand it over, bub," George instructed.

Mr Krupp unlocked a large filing cabinet and opened the bottom drawer. He reached in and handed George the videotape. George stuffed it into his backpack.

Harold took a *different* video out of his backpack and put it into the file cabinet.

"What's that video?" asked George.

"It's one of my little sister's old 'Boomer the Purple Dragon Sing-A-Long' videos."

"Nice touch," said George.

CHAPTER 11
FUN WITH HYPNOSIS

When Harold bent down to close the filing cabinet, he took a quick look inside.

"Whoa!" he cried. "Look at all the stuff in here!"

The filing cabinet was filled with everything Mr Krupp had taken away from the boys over the years. There were slingshots, whoopee cushions, skateboards, fake doggy doo-doo – you name it, it was in there.

"Look at this!" cried George. "A big stack of *Captain Underpants* comics!"

"He's got every issue!" said Harold.

For hours, the two boys sat on the floor laughing and reading their comics. Finally, George looked up at the clock.

"Yikes!" he said. "It's almost lunchtime! We better clean up this mess and get to class."

The boys looked up at their principal, who had been standing behind them in a trance all morning.

"Gee, I almost forgot about Mr Krupp," said Harold. "What should we do with him?"

"Do you want to have some fun?" asked George.

"Why not?" said Harold. "I haven't had *any* fun in the last four-to-six weeks!"

"Cool," said George. He walked up to Mr Krupp and snapped his fingers. *Snap!* "You are – a *chicken*!" he said.

Suddenly, Mr Krupp leaped on to his desk and flapped his arms "Cluck, cluck, cluck-cluck," he cried, kicking his papers off the desk behind him and pecking at his pen-and-pencil set.

George and Harold howled with laughter.

"Let me try, let me try," said Harold.

"Ummm, you are a – a *monkey*!"

"You gotta snap your fingers," said George.

"Oh, yeah," said Harold. *Snap!* "You are a *monkey*!"

Suddenly, Mr Krupp sprang off his desk and began swinging from the fluorescent light fixtures. "Ooo-ooo, ooo-oooo, OOOOO!" he shrieked, leaping from one side of the room to the other.

George and Harold laughed so hard they almost cried.

"My turn, my turn!" said George. "Let's see. What should we turn him into next?"

"I know," Harold said, holding up a *Captain Underpants* comic. "Let's turn him into Captain Underpants!"

"Good idea," said George. *Snap!* "You are now the greatest superhero of all time: *The Amazing Captain Underpants*!"

Mr Krupp tore down the red curtain from his office window and tied it around his neck. Then he took off his shoes, socks, shirt, trousers, and his awful toupee.

"Tra-La-Laaaaaaaa!" he sang.

Mr Krupp stood before them looking
quite triumphant, with his cape blowing
in the breeze of the open window. George
and Harold were dumbfounded.

"You know," said George, "he kinda
looks like Captain Underpants."

"Yeah," Harold replied.

After a short silence, the two boys
looked at each other and burst into
laughter. George and Harold had never
laughed so hard in all their lives. Tears
ran down their faces as they rolled about
the floor, shrieking in hysterics.

After a while, George pulled himself up
from the floor for another look.

"Hey," George cried. "Where'd he go?"

CHAPTER 12
OUT OF THE WINDOW

George and Harold dashed to the window and looked out. There, running across the car park, was a pudgy old guy in his underwear with a red cape flowing behind him.

"Mr Krupp, come back!" shouted Harold.

"He won't answer to *that*," said George. "He thinks he's Captain Underpants now."

"Oh, no," said Harold.

"He's probably runnin' off to fight crime," said George.

"Oh, *no,*" said Harold.

"And we gotta stop him," said George.

"Oh, NO," cried Harold. *"NO WAY!"*

"Look," said George, "he could get *killed* out there."

Harold was unmoved.

"Or worse," said George. "We could get into BIG trouble!"

"You're right," said Harold. "We *gotta* go after him!"

The two boys opened the bottom cabinet drawer and took out their slingshots and skateboards.

"Do you think we should bring anything else?" asked Harold.

"Yeah," said George. "Let's bring the fake doggy doo-doo."

"Good thinking," said Harold. "You just never know when fake doggy doo-doo is going to come in handy!"

Harold stuffed Mr Krupp's clothes, shoes and toupee into his backpack. Then together the two boys leaped out the window, slid down the flagpole, and took off on their skateboards after the Amazing Captain Underpants.

CHAPTER 13
BANK ROBBERS

George and Harold rode their skateboards all over town looking for Captain Underpants.

"I can't find him anywhere," said Harold.

"You'd think a guy like him would be *easy* to spot," said George.

Then the boys turned a corner, and *there* he was. Captain Underpants was standing in front of a bank, looking quite heroic.

"Mr Krupp!" cried Harold.

"Shhh," said George, "don't call him that. Call him Captain Underpants!"

"Oh, yeah," said Harold.

"And don't forget to snap your fingers," said George.

"Right!" said Harold.

RRRRiiiiNNNC

ALARM

But before he got a chance, the bank doors flew wide open, and out stepped two robbers. The robbers took one look at Captain Underpants and stopped dead in their tracks.

"Surrender!" said Captain Underpants. "Or I will have to resort to *Wedgie Power*!"

"Oh, no," whispered Harold and George.

Nobody moved for about ten seconds. Finally, the robbers looked at each other and burst out laughing. They dropped their loot and fell to the pavement screaming in hysterics.

Almost immediately, the cops arrived and arrested the crooks.

"Let that be a lesson to you," cried Captain Underpants. "Never underestimate the power of underwear!"

The police chief, looking quite angry, marched over to Captain Underpants.

"And just who the heck are *you* supposed to be?" the police chief demanded.

"Why, *I'm* Captain Underpants, the world's greatest superhero," said Captain Underpants. "I fight for Truth, Justice, and *all* that is Pre-Shrunk and Cottony!"

"Oh, *YEAH*!!?" shouted the police chief. "Cuff him, boys!"

One of the cops took out his handcuffs and grabbed Captain Underpants by the arm.

"Uh-oh!" cried George. "We gotta roll!"
Together the two boys zoomed into the
crowd, weaving in and out of cops and
bystanders. Harold skated up to Captain
Underpants and knocked the superhero
off his feet. George caught him and the
boys skated away with Captain
Underpants on their shoulders.

"Stop!" cried the cops, but it was too
late. George, Harold, and Captain
Underpants were gone.

CHAPTER 14
THE BIG BANG

After their quick escape, George, Harold, and Captain Underpants stopped on a deserted street corner to catch their breath.

"OK," said George. "Let's de-hypnotize him quick, before something else. . .

. . .happens!"

A huge explosion came from the Rare Crystal Shop across the street. Heavy smoke poured out of the building. Suddenly, two robots with one stolen crystal emerged from the smoke and jumped into an old van.

"Did I just see two *ROBOTS* get into a van?" asked Harold.

"You know," said George, "up until *now* this story was almost *believable*!"

"Well, believable or not," said Harold, "we're not getting involved. I repeat: We are *NOT* getting involved!"

Just then, Captain Underpants leaped from the street corner and dashed in front of the van.

"Stop, in the name of underwear!" he cried.

"Uh-oh," said George. "I think we're *involved*."

The two robots started up the van and swerved around Captain Underpants. Unfortunately, the van brushed up against his red cape, and it got caught. With a mighty *jerk*, Captain Underpants flipped backwards, and the van pulled him along as it drove away.

THE BAD GUYS!

"GRAB HIM!" cried George.

The two boys skateboarded with all their might towards the speeding van and grabbed Captain Underpants by the ankles.

"HEEEEEEELLLLLLLP!" they cried as the van pulled them through the city streets.

"Mommy," said a little boy sitting on a bench, "I just saw two robots driving a van with a guy in his underwear hanging off the back by a red cape, pulling two boys on skateboards behind him with his feet."

"How do you expect me to believe such a ridiculous story?" asked his mother.

Finally, the van came to a screeching halt in front of an old abandoned warehouse. The sudden stop made Captain Underpants flip over the roof of the van and crash through the front door of the building.

"Well, well, well," said a strange voice from inside the warehouse. "It looks as if we have a *visitor*."

CHAPTER 15
DR NAPPY

George and Harold hid behind the van
until the coast was clear. Then they
sneaked up to the hole in the door and
peeked inside.

Captain Underpants was all tied up,
the two robots were standing guard, and
a strange little man wearing a nappy was
laughing maniacally.

"I am the evil Dr Nappy," the strange little man told Captain Underpants. "And you will be the first to witness my takeover of the *world*!"

Dr Nappy placed the stolen crystal into a large machine called the *Laser-Matic 2000*. The machine started to light up and make loud noises. Heavy gears began shifting and spinning, and a laser beam from the crystal shot straight up through a hole in the roof.

"In exactly twenty minutes, this laser beam will blow up the moon and send huge chunks of it crashing down upon every major city in the world!" laughed Dr Nappy. "Then, I will rise from the rubble and take over the planet!"

"Only one thing can help us now," said George.

"What?" asked Harold.

"Rubber doggy doo-doo," said George.

Harold took the fake doggy doo-doo and a slingshot from George's backpack and handed them to him.

"Be careful," said Harold. "The fate of the entire planet is in your hands!"

With careful and precise aim, George shot the rubber doo-doo through the air and across the room. It landed with a *plop*! – right at the feet of Dr Nappy.

"Yessss!" whispered George and Harold.

Dr Nappy looked down at the doo-doo between his feet and turned bright red.

"Oh, dear me!" he cried. "I'm dreadfully embarrassed! Please excuse me."

He began to waddle towards the toilet. "This has never happened to me before, I assure you," he said. "I-I guess with all the excitement, I just . . . I just . . . Oh, dear! Oh, dear!"

While Dr Nappy was off changing himself, George and Harold sneaked into the old warehouse.

Immediately, the robots detected the boys and began marching towards them. "Destroy the intruders!" said the robots. "Destroy the intruders!"

George and Harold screamed and ran to the back of the warehouse. Luckily, George found two old boards and gave one of them to Harold.

"We're not going to have to resort to extremely graphic violence, are we?" asked Harold.

"I sure hope not," said George.

CHAPTER 16
THE EXTREMELY GRAPHIC
VIOLENCE CHAPTER

WARNING:

The following chapter contains graphic scenes showing two boys beating the tar out of a couple of robots.

If you have high blood pressure, or if you faint at the sight of motor oil, we strongly urge you to take better care of yourself and stop being such a baby.

As everybody knows, nothing enhances silly action sequences more than really cheesy animation.

And so, for the first time in the history of great literature, we proudly bring you the latest in cheesy animation technology: TThe art of FLIP-O-RAMA!

PILKEY® BRAND
O-RAMA

HERE'S HOW IT WORKS!

Step 1
Place your *left* hand inside the dotted lines marked "LEFT HAND HERE". Hold the book open *flat*.

Step 2
Grasp the *right-hand* page with your right thumb and index finger (inside the dotted lines marked "RIGHT THUMB HERE").

Step 3
Now *quickly* flip the right-hand page back and forth until the picture appears to be *animated*.

(For extra fun, try adding your own sound-effects!)

FLIP-O-RAMA 1

(pages 87 and 89)

Remember, flip *only* page 87.
While you are flipping, be sure you
can see the picture on page 87
and the one on page 89.
If you flip quickly, the two
pictures will start to look like
one *animated* picture.

Don't forget to
add your own sound-effects!

LEFT HAND HERE

ROBOT RAMPAGE!

RIGHT
THUMB
HERE

ROBOT RAMPAGE!

FLIP-O-RAMA 2

(pages 91 and 93)

Remember, flip *only* page 91.
While you are flipping, be sure you
can see the picture on page 91
and the one on page 93.
If you flip quickly, the two
pictures will start to look like
<u>one</u> *animated* picture.

Don't forget to
add your own sound-effects!

LEFT HAND HERE

GEORGE SAVES
HAROLD!

RIGHT
THUMB
HERE

GEORGE SAVES HAROLD!

FLIP-O-RAMA 3

(pages 95 and 97)

Remember, flip *only* page 95.
While you are flipping, be sure you
can see the picture on page 95
and the one on page 97.
If you flip quickly, the two
pictures will start to look like
<u>one</u> *animated* picture.

Don't forget to
add your own sound-effects!

LEFT HAND HERE

HAROLD RETURNS
THE FAVOUR!

RIGHT
INDEX
FINGER
HERE

96

HAROLD RETURNS
THE FAVOUR!

FLIP-O-RAMA 4

(pages 99 and 101)

Remember, flip *only* page 99.
While you are flipping, be sure you
can see the picture on page 99
and the one on page 101.
If you flip quickly, the two
pictures will start to look like
~~one~~ *animated* picture.

Don't forget to
add your own sound-effects!

LEFT HAND HERE

MIXED NUTS
(...AND BOLTS!)

RIGHT
THUMB
HERE

MIXED NUTS
(...AND BOLTS!)

CHAPTER 17
THE ESCAPE

After defeating the robots, George and Harold untied Captain Underpants.

"Come on!" cried Harold. "Let's get out of here!"

"Wait!" said Captain Underpants. "We have to save the world first!"

So George, Harold, and Captain Underpants frantically looked all over the *Laser-Matic 2000*, searching for a way to shut it down and stop the inevitable disaster.

"Ummm," said Harold. "I think *this* might be the lever we want."

He pulled the "Self-Destruct" lever with all his might. Suddenly, the *Laser-Matic 2000* began to sputter and shake. The huge laser beam turned off, and pieces of the machine began flying off in all directions.

"It's gonna BLOW!" cried Harold. "RUN FOR YOUR LIVES!"

"*NOT SO FAST!*" screamed Dr Nappy, who had appeared out of nowhere. "You demolished my robots. You *destroyed* my *Laser-Matic 2000*. And you ruined my one chance to take over the world – but you won't live to tell the tale!" Dr Nappy pulled out his *Nappy-Matic 2000* ray gun, and pointed it at George, Harold and Captain Underpants.

Captain Underpants quickly stretched a pair of underwear and shot it at Dr Nappy. The underwear landed right on the evil doctor's head.

"Help!" cried Dr Nappy. "I can't see! I can't see!"

George and Harold ran out of the
warehouse as fast as they could.

"Great shot, Captain Underpants!"
cried Harold.

"There's just one thing I don't
understand," said George. "Where'd
you get the *extra* pair of underwear?"

"What extra pair?" said Captain
Underpants.

"Never mind that," cried George, "let's just get out of here before that *Laser-Matic 2000* thing ex. . .

. . .plodes!"

The *Laser-Matic 2000* blew up, tearing apart the old warehouse. It sent flaming shards of red-hot metal in every direction. Fire fell from the skies around our heroes, and the earth began to crumble beneath their feet.

"Oh, NO!" cried Harold. *"WE'RE DOOMED!"*

CHAPTER 18
TO MAKE A LONG
STORY SHORT

They got away.

CHAPTER 19
BACK TO SCHOOL

George, Harold and Captain Underpants
made a quick stop outside the police
station. They tied Dr Nappy to a lamppost
and attached a note to him.

"There!" said Captain Underpants.
"That ought to explain everything."

Then George and Harold led Captain
Underpants back to Jerome Horwitz
Elementary School.

"Why are we going *here*?" asked
Captain Underpants.

"Well," said George, "you have to do
some *undercover* work here."

"Yeah," said Harold, reaching into his
backpack. "Put these clothes on, and
make it snappy!"

"Don't forget your hair," said George.

Captain Underpants quickly got
dressed behind some bushes. "Well, how
do I look?" he asked.

"Pretty good," said George. "Now try
to look really angry!"

Captain Underpants made the nastiest
face he could.

"You know," said Harold, "he kinda
looks like Mr Krupp!"

"*Harold,*" whispered George, "he *is*
Mr Krupp!"

"Oh, yeah," said Harold. "I almost
forgot."

Before long, they were all back inside Mr Krupp's office.

"OK, Captain Underpants," said George, "you are now Mr Krupp."

"Snap your fingers," whispered Harold.

"Oh, yeah," said George. *Snap!* "You are now Mr Krupp."

"Who's Mr Krupp?" asked Captain Underpants.

"Oh, NO!" cried Harold. *"It's not working!"*

The boys tried again and again to de-hypnotize Captain Underpants, but *nothing* seemed to work.

116

"Hmmm," said Harold. "Let me see the instruction manual for that ring."

George checked his trousers pockets.

"Umm," said George, "I think I *lost* it."

"You WHAT?" cried Harold. The two boys searched frantically through the office, but the 3-D Hypno-Ring instruction manual was nowhere to be found.

"Never mind," said George. "I have an idea." He removed the flowers from a large vase in the corner. Then he poured out all of the water over Captain Underpants's head.

"What did you do *that* for?" cried Harold.

"I saw 'em do this in a cartoon once," said George, "so it's *gotta* work!"

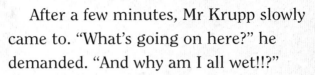

After a few minutes, Mr Krupp slowly came to. "What's going on here?" he demanded. "And why am I all wet!!?"

George and Harold had never been so glad to see Mr Krupp in all their lives.

"I'm so happy I could cry," said Harold.

"Well, you're *gonna* cry when I give that videotape to the football team!" shouted Mr Krupp. "I've *had it* with you two!"

Principal Krupp took the videotape
out of his filing cabinet. "You boys are
dead meat!" he sneered. He stormed out
of his office with the video and headed
towards the gym.

George and Harold smiled. "Wait'll the
football team sees *that* video!" said
Harold.

"Yeah," said George, "I sure hope they
like singing purple dragons!"

"Hey, look," said George. "I found the 3-D Hypno-Ring instruction manual. It was in my *shirt* pocket, not my trousers pocket!"

"Well, throw that thing away," said Harold. "We'll never need it again."

"I sure hope not," said George.

WARNING!!!
Whatever you do, don't pour water on anybody's head when they are in a trance! This will cause the hypnotized person to slip back and forth from trance to reality whenever they hear the sound of fingers snapping.

TRASH

CHAPTER 20
THE END?

LA-LA-LA-LA- WE LOVE BOOMER-LA-LA

PURPLE DRAGON SING-A-LONG FRIENDS

Things at Jerome Horwitz Elementary School were never quite the same after that fateful day.

The football team enjoyed Mr Krupp's video so much that they changed their name from the Knuckleheads to the Purple Dragon Sing-A-Long Friends. The name change didn't go over too well with the fans, but hey, who's going to argue with a bunch of linebackers?

George and Harold went back to their old ways, pulling pranks, cracking jokes, and making new comic books.

They had to keep an eye on Mr Krupp, though. . .

. . .because for some *strange* reason,
every time he heard the sound of fingers
snapping. . .

Snap!

. . .Principal Krupp turned *back* into. . .

. . .*you know who*!

"Oh, no!" cried Harold.
"Here we go *again*!" said George.

The ORIGIN of CAPTAIN UNDERPANTS

Dav Pilkey created Captain Underpants
when he was eight years old. It all
happened back in 1974, when Dav was
a second grader at St John's Lutheran
School in Elyria, Ohio. It might not
surprise you to know that Dav Pilkey
was the class clown back in the second
grade. He was also the class artist.

Whenever Dav got a chance, he would draw funny pictures to make his friends laugh. Dav also folded sheets of paper in half to make his own Flip-O-Ramas, which depicted ridiculous scenes of mayhem (he and his friends called them "Flip-Actions" back then). Like George and Harold, Dav Pilkey even made his own original comic books. All of these things were seen as great distractions and annoyances by Dav's cantankerous teacher, Ms Ribble.*

*not her real name

It was this very teacher, however, who inadvertently gave Dav the idea for Captain Underpants. One day, Ms Ribble was talking to the class and she happened to use the word *underwear*. Everyone in Dav's class immediately began to laugh. This irritated Dav's teacher, and she got very angry.

She scolded the children, shouting:

This only made the class laugh even harder. At that moment, Dav Pilkey had an epiphany. He realized that underwear was a very powerful thing. Just the mere mention of it could make everyone laugh.

That day, Dav Pilkey drew his very first

drawing of a caped hero named Captain
Underpants. Dav's drawing was an
immediate hit with his classmates. Ms
Ribble, however, was not amused. She
immediately tore up Dav's drawing and
sent him out into the hallway.

Dav Pilkey was no stranger to spending time in the hallway. In the second grade, Dav got banished to the hallway almost every day. Usually, he spent this time sneaking up and down the corridors, changing the letters on all of the bulletin boards around so that they spelled out

MISTER PILKEY, OUT!

ridiculous things. It wasn't long before Ms
Ribble got wise to Dav's hallway
shenanigans, and moved a spare desk
out there so he would stay put.

Usually, Dav just drew silly pictures
while he sat at his hallway desk. But on
the day of Dav's great epiphany, he was
inspired. He began making a comic book
about his underwear-clad hero. Captain
Underpants flew into action on the pages

of Dav's story, defeating terrible monsters, rescuing innocent children and saving the world in crazy Flip-Action scenes.

When Dav was finally allowed back into the classroom, he brought his comic book in with him. It didn't take long before Captain Underpants's first adventure began causing outbursts of laughter and

hysteria. Ms Ribble seized Dav's comic, ripped it up, and told him he'd better straighten up. "You can't spend the rest of your life making silly books," she told him.

Despite his teacher's admonishments, Dav Pilkey did indeed continue making silly books. In fact, Dav got his very first silly book *published* when he was still in college.

After he graduated, Dav wrote and illustrated many more silly books about

dogs, cats, mice, dragons, and dumb
bunnies. When he wasn't making books,
Dav visited hundreds of schools and
libraries and talked with children about
his experiences as an author.

Every time Dav spoke, he would draw
a giant picture of Captain Underpants,
which made the children laugh hysterically.
At the end of his presentations, kids would
always ask Dav the same question: "Are
you ever going to make a book about
Captain Underpants?"

"I don't know," Dav would reply. "Do you think I should?" The answer was always a resounding, roof-raising scream of. . .

So in 1996, Dav Pilkey began writing and drawing the book you are holding in your hands right now. Dav wanted to include as much of his own childhood as possible in the book, so he based George and Harold on himself. Like Dav, George and Harold are class clowns *AND* class artists. They make comics, they switch letters around on signs, and they are always getting in trouble with their teachers and principal for one thing or another.

. . .And of course, their action scenes are always presented in Flip-O-Rama.

FUN FACT #1

George and Harold got their names from two famous children's books that Dav Pilkey loved as a child: *Curious George* and *Harold and the Purple Crayon*.

FUN FACT #2

George's and Harold's last names, Beard and Hutchins, were the last names of two child actors who appeared in Hal Roach's *Our Gang* comedies (also known as *The Little Rascals*). Dav watched that show every day when he was a kid, and his two favorite characters, Wheezer and Stymie, were portrayed by child actors Bobby Hutchins and Matthew Beard.

FUN FACT #3

Mr Krupp's last name was also taken from an *Our Gang/Little Rascals* character (sort of). The 1934 short film, *Shrimps for a Day*, featured an evil, grouchy old man who made quite an impression on Dav when he was a kid. The character's name in the film was "Mr Crutch," but Dav remembered it incorrectly, instead giving Captain Underpants's alter ego the moniker "Mr Krupp". If Dav Pilkey's memory had been better, Mr Krupp would have been called "Mr Crutch".

FUN FACT #4

Jerome Horwitz Elementary School was named after "Curly", one of the Three Stooges (another show Dav Pilkey watched every day as a child). Curly's real name was Jerome Horwitz.

FUN FACT #5

Dav Pilkey not only writes all of the Captain Underpants stories, he also does all of the illustrations (including the paintings on the covers). It takes Dav about six months to write each book, and another six months to draw and paint every picture.

FUN FACT #6

Dav draws all of the interior illustrations with pencil. They are then photocopied on to white card stock and painted with watercolor paint. The covers are painted in acrylics with a dash of India ink.

HAVE YOU READ YOUR UNDERPANTS TODAY?

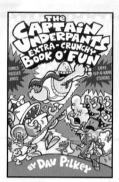

ABOUT THE AUTHOR

When Dav Pilkey was a kid, his teachers thought he was disruptive, "behaviorally challenged," and in serious need of a major attitude adjustment.

When he wasn't writing sentences in the detention room, he could usually be found sitting at his private desk out in the hallway. There he spent his time writing and drawing his own original comic books about a superhero named Captain Underpants.